THE Little House by the Sea

BENEDICT BLATHWAYT

TACKLE & BOOKS

TOBERMORY

For John and Anne Forrester

First published in
Great Britain in 2015 by
BC Books an imprint of
Birlinn Ltd
West Newington House
10 Newington Road
Edinburgh EH9 1QS

www.birlinn.co.uk

in association with

Tackle and Books
6–8 Main Street, Tobermory
Isle of Mull PA75 6NU

www.tackleandbooks.co.uk

Parts of this book were first published as
The Little House by the Sea by Julia MacRae Books in 1992

ISBN: 978 1 78027 314 3

British Library Cataloguing-in-Publication Data
A catalogue record for this book is available from the British Library

Designed by Mark Blackadder

Printed and bound by Livonia, Latvia

Once there was a little house by the sea.

Its door was gone and its windows were empty.

It belonged to nobody.

But mice lived snug and dry in the rough stone walls.

Rabbits nibbled sweet weeds in the overgrown garden.

Sheep sheltered from the rain in the doorway.

Sparrows flew in and out of the broken windows
and nested under the roof.

A stray cat came to sleep in the fireplace.

And a lonely seagull liked to perch high on the
chimney stack and look out to sea.

But one day a fisherman called Finn came to the little house . . .

. . . and began to change everything.

He mended the roof and made a new door.

He fitted new windows.

He filled in the cracks in the wall with cement,
and weeded the garden.

And then he lit a roaring fire in the fireplace.

He lived in the little house now. And as soon as the cement
was hard and the paint had dried and the little house by the sea
stood all new and bright and finished . . .

. . . Finn the fisherman set off to do some fishing.

He caught some fine lobsters in his lobster pots,

and lots of slippery silver mackerel on a long fishing line.

And then Finn picked up a group of holidaymakers
and took them on a boat trip.

He steered his boat between some sharp rocks so that
everyone could get really close to the seals.

Then they landed on a little island. Finn showed the
holidaymakers a huge cave, and told them about a
giant called Fingal who had lived there long ago.

Afterwards they climbed up to the top of the
cliffs to watch the puffins.

Soon it was time for Finn to take the holidaymakers back.
Goodbye, puffins! Goodbye, seals!

Then Finn set off home to his brand new little house by the sea.
But what about all the animals who had lived there before him?
Had they been forgotten? Did they live somewhere else now?

No! When Finn got home, he gave the cat some milk.

He fed the sparrows.

He let the sheep shelter in his shed, and pretended not
to see the naughty rabbits in his garden.

And he didn't really mind that the mice
had found a new way into his house.

Even the seagull was happy. The little house
by the sea had a place for everyone.